Why the Sky Is Far Away

Why Thunder Chases Lightning

Why Sun and Moon Live in the Sky

THREE POURQUOI TALES FROM AFRICA

retold by Cynthia Swain
illustrated by Gerardo Suzán

Table of Contents

POURQUOI TALES

What is a pourquoi tale?

A pourquoi tale is a short story that explains why something in the natural world is the way it is. Usually the characters in a pourquoi tale are animals. Sometimes the characters are other objects in nature, such as the sun, the sky, or the sea.

What is the purpose of a pourquoi tale?

Pourquoi tales are explanations of why and how things happen in nature. Pourquoi tales allow us to think about what caused the curious things we see in the world. Pourquoi tales often point out character flaws, or foibles, that people have, such as being boastful, proud, or impatient. In addition, these tales entertain us.

How do you read a pourquoi tale?

When you read a pourquoi tale, pay attention to the title. The title will help you know what question the story answers. Pay attention to the actions of the main characters as well. These actions will cause some type of change in nature. Think about how the events in the tale explain why something is the way it is.

Features of a Pourquoi Tale

The setting is often a key part of the story.

The story is brief. The title is about something in nature.

The main characters are usually animals or objects in nature.

The story presents a problem and a solution that explains why things in nature are a certain way.

The characters' actions cause something to occur, or happen, in nature.

One character has a flaw.

Who invented pourquoi tales?

People have told pourquoi tales for tens of thousands of years. Many ancient cultures, including the Greeks, Chinese, and Egyptians, used these types of stories to explain nature and the universe. Many Native American, African, and Asian storytellers also used these tales to answer questions about the world, such as:

• Why do certain animals look and act the way they do?
• How did Earth, the sun, and the moon come to be?
• Why do the seasons change?

Today, some authors still use this genre to explain events in nature in a fun and imaginative way.

Learn About

AFRICAN STORYTELLERS

Who were the African storytellers? Tribes throughout Africa told pourquoi tales. Children were often taught to tell stories as a part of their education and to help them become members of the community. In some tribes, official storytellers, or griots (GREE-oh), were responsible for passing on the history, culture, values, and wisdom of the village. Many griots used music, dance, costumes, and props to help tell their stories.

What were the stories about? Many stories were about animals that talked, thought, and acted like humans. Listeners laughed at and learned from these stories. Pourquoi tales provided the listeners with problem-solving strategies and encouraged them to use their wits in their daily challenges.

Why do we still know the stories today? The stories were passed down through the generations from one storyteller to the next. Stories often changed a bit with each retelling as people forgot or added details, changed the characters' names, and adapted the stories to their own lives. Stories also changed as people told them in different languages. For example, even today, hundreds of languages are spoken in Nigeria, the country in western Africa where these three tales originated.

a modern-day griot

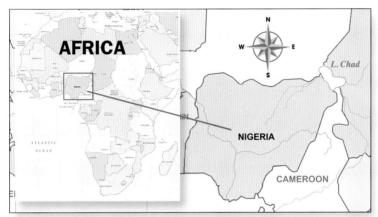

The stories in this book are from tribes in western Africa.

Tools Writers Use

Simile

Look at the word **simile** (SIH-muh-lee). Does it remind you of the word **similar**? Things that are similar are alike in some way. Most similes compare two things using the words **like** or **as**. Writers use similes to describe how characters look and act so that readers can create vivid pictures in their minds. In these pourquoi tales, notice how the author uses similes to compare the characters' traits to familiar objects, particularly those in nature.

Why the Sky Is Far Away

Long ago, rain did not fall from the sky. The wind did not blow. The sun did not rise or set. The sky was close to the ground. People could touch the sky.

Best of all, the sky was made of food. People could take a piece of sky any time. They could eat any time. Some said the sky tasted like corn. Others said the sky was as sweet as sugar.

People did not need to work then. There were no farmers. There were no hunters. People spent their time painting. They sang. They played games. Most people were happy to share the sky. But a few people were not **content**. They were as greedy as thieves. They took big pieces of sky. They ate just a little. Then they threw away the rest.

The sky grew unhappy. People were wasting his gifts. Tears filled his eyes. He called for the king.

The king raced to the sky. He went to see what was the **matter**. "Oh kind and mighty Sky, what is the problem?"

Sky said, "I have been good to the people for many years. I have asked for only one thing in return: Do not waste the sky. There will not be enough food. I will not be able to feed all the people."

"I have told the people to be careful," said the king. "Most have listened. But some people have not. I will tell them again."

The king bowed. He showed the sky respect.

"Thank you," said Sky.

The king called his people together. "Never take more sky than you can eat. It is a gift. If you waste it, the sky will fly away," he said. "We have one more chance."

The people said they would be careful. One group did not. They did not listen to anyone. They still ate like pigs.

"Let the others be like sheep," said this group. "We will do what we want. The sky will not know."

That night, the group of piggy people took one mile of the sky. They ate just a **minute** bit. They buried the rest behind their home.

The sky saw what this group did. He got angry. His voice boomed like thunder.

"You have not listened. I will leave this world. I will take the sun. I will take the moon. I will take the clouds with me into space," he said.

The king was sad. He was upset.

"Please don't leave us," he begged the sky.

The sky was mad. But he also felt bad. He knew that many good people were on Earth.

"I will let the sun, moon, and clouds stay behind. But I must go away. From now on, people must learn to plant. They must hunt for food. They must learn to fish."

So the sky floated up. It went into space. That is where it is today. And that is why the sky is far away.

Reread the Pourquoi Tale

Analyze the Characters, Setting, and Plot

- Where does the story take place? When does it take place?
- Who are the main characters in the story? How would you describe each character?
- What caused the sky to leave? Do you think he did the right thing? Why or why not?
- What question does the tale answer?

Analyze the Tools Writers Use: Simile

- Why did the author use the following similes to describe the taste of the sky: "Some said that the sky tasted like corn. Others said the sky was as sweet as sugar."
- Why did the author use two animal similes to compare people: "They still ate like pigs." "'Let the others be like sheep,' said this group."

Focus on Words: Multiple Meanings

Words that sound the same but have different meanings are multiple-meaning words. Sometimes, a word can even be a noun in one meaning and a verb in another. Below are multiple-meaning words from the story. Make a chart like the one below. Then use context clues to help you figure out which meaning is correct in the tale.

Word	But a few people were not **content**.	He went to see what was the **matter**.	They ate just a **minute** bit.
Meaning #1			
Meaning #2			
Correct meaning?			
How do you know?			

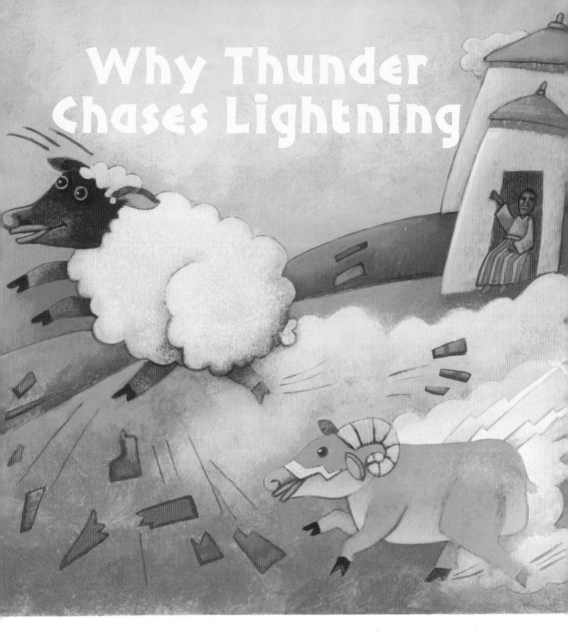

Why Thunder Chases Lightning

Long ago, Thunder and Lightning lived with people. They lived in a village on Earth. Thunder was an old mother sheep. Her son Lightning was a ram. They often made trouble. One day, the king asked them to move. "Go to the far end of the village," the king said. "Go far from the homes of the people."

But there was no peace. Lightning had a bad temper. When he got mad, he set fire to the huts. He knocked down trees like a bull in a china shop. Sometimes he burned the farms. Sometimes he hurt people. Whenever Lightning was bad, Thunder got as mad as a hornet. She would call to Lightning in a loud, crackling voice. Her voice shook the ground. Her voice made people shake like leaves. She yelled at Lightning. She tried to scare him. Lightning did not care. Then Thunder would chase Lightning. She chased him all night long. They made an awful **racket**. At last, the people could not **stand** it any longer. The people complained to the king.

The king told Thunder to leave the village. He told Lightning to leave. He made them move far away. They moved to the bushes.

This did not help. Lightning still got mad. He burned the forests. Now the land was as flat as a pancake. The fire spread to the farms. The farms burned, too.

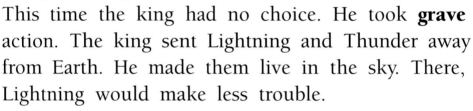

The people complained again. This time the king had no choice. He took **grave** action. The king sent Lightning and Thunder away from Earth. He made them live in the sky. There, Lightning would make less trouble.

Thunder stayed mad at her son. To this day, when Lightning is mad, he lights up the sky. He sets fire to Earth. And you can hear Thunder chasing him. She is calling after him in the distance.

Reread the Pourquoi Tale

Analyze the Characters, Setting, and Plot

- Where did the tale take place? Why is this setting important?
- Why did the people complain to the king?
- Which characters had flaws? Did the characters learn a lesson?
- What question does the tale answer?

Analyze the Tools Writers Use: Simile

Find examples of similes in the story when . . .

- Lightning knocks down trees. (page 13)
- Thunder gets angry at her son. (page 13)
- Thunder's voice frightens people. (page 13)
- Lightning burns the forests. (page 14)

Focus on Words: Multiple Meanings

Make a chart like the one below. Then use context clues to help you figure out which meaning is correct in the tale.

Word	They made an awful **racket**.	The people could not **stand** it any longer.	He took **grave** action.
Meaning #1			
Meaning #2			
Correct meaning?			
How do you know?			

Why Sun and Moon Live in the Sky

This story is from the beginning of time. Sun, Moon, and Water lived on Earth. Sun had a beautiful house. It twinkled like a star. Moon's home was a shining silver castle. Water's home was wide open. It was as blue as the sky.

Every day, Sun visited Water. She always brought a **present**. Her best gift was a sunny day. Sun was a thoughtful friend.

A few weeks went by. Sun wondered, "Where is Water? Where is *my* present? I would love to have a pet dolphin. Haven't I been a good friend to Water?"

Sun decided to **address** her friend. She called out, "Why don't you visit, Water? Is something wrong with my home?"

"No, not really," said Water. "But your house is too small for me. Don't forget: The largest animals in the world live with me. My whales are as big as your house, my dear friend."

"I see," said Sun. "I will fix that. I will make my house bigger. Give me a few days. Then come to see me."

The author begins the story with a description of the setting, which is often an important part of a pourquoi tale.

The main characters in the story are objects in nature, but they can talk and act like human beings. This is another feature of pourquoi tales.

Now that the author has established the setting and main characters, she introduces the problem of the story: Sun's house is not big enough to hold Water.

The author uses a simile to compare Sun and Moon's hard work to that of busy bees. This simile also shows that Sun and Moon are kind, caring characters.

Sun went home. She talked with Moon. Soon, they were as busy as bees. They worked hand in hand to build a home. The new home was as large as Earth itself.

Finally, Water came to visit. She knocked on Sun's door. "Is it safe to come in? Is there room for me and all my animals?"

"Yes" said Sun. "Please come in. Sit down. Moon is also here."

"Welcome," said Moon.

As the story develops, the author makes the problem grow worse. Now, Water is taking over Sun's new home. Sun and Moon's "flaw" is that they have not planned well for Water's visit.

Water quickly rushed in. A million small fish came in. Sun and Moon were soon knee deep in water.

"So, how are you both?" asked Water. "Are you glad to see me?"

"Oh, yes," said Sun and Moon. "Our feet are wet. But it is so great to have you back. Who are all your friends?"

More water poured in. Along came sharks, bass, and sea birds. As quick as a wink, Sun and Moon were soaked. Water was up to their necks.

"Oh no!" said Water. She was upset. "I can't let the rivers in. There are too many boats. You might drown."

Finally, toward the end of the story, the author solves the problem. The dialogue and actions of Sun and Moon fit their kind character, which the author established earlier in the story.

Because this is a pourquoi tale, it ends with an explanation of the title.

"We will be fine," said Sun and Moon. "We'll climb to the roof."

So the rivers and boats flowed in. Sun and Moon **rose** far above the roof. They had no choice. They flew like birds into the sky. But they could never return to their flooded homes. That is why Sun and Moon live in the sky.

20

Reread the Pourquoi Tale

Analyze the Characters, Setting, and Plot

- Where did the tale take place? Why is this setting important?
- Why did Sun want Water to visit?
- Were any of the characters unkind? Explain your answer.
- What question does the tale answer?

Analyze the Tools Writers Use: Simile

Find examples of similes in the story.

- Water's home was . . . (page 17)
- Sun talked with Moon. Soon, they were . . . (page 18)
- . . . Sun and Moon were soaked. (page 19)
- They flew . . . into the sky. (page 20)

Focus on Words: Multiple Meanings

Make a chart like the one below. Then use context clues to help you figure out which meaning is correct in the tale.

Word	She always brought a **present**.	Sun decided to **address** her friend.	Sun and Moon **rose** far above the roof.
Meaning #1			
Meaning #2			
Correct meaning?			
How do you know?			

How does an author write a

POURQUOI TALE?

Reread "Why Sun and Moon Live in the Sky" and think about what the author did to write this tale. How did she develop the story line? How can you, as a writer, develop your own tale?

1. ## Decide on a Question about Nature
Remember, a pourquoi tale answers a question about animals or other parts of nature. In "Why Sun and Moon Live in the Sky," the author wanted to give an explanation of why we have a sun and a moon in the sky.

2. ## Brainstorm Characters
Writers ask these questions:
- Who is my main character?
- What human flaw does my main character have?
- How does my main character show this flaw? What does he or she do, say, or think?
- What other character will be important to my story? How will this character show that he or she does not have the flaw of the main character?

Character	Water	Sun and Moon
Traits	responsible; polite	generous; good friends
Flaw/Asset	bigger than she thinks	want to help Water, but don't plan well
Examples	floods Sun and Moon out of their homes on Earth	make room for Water, but have to move away

3. Brainstorm Setting and Plot
Writers ask these questions:
- Where does my pourquoi tale take place? How will I describe it?
- What is the problem, or situation?
- What events happen?
- How does the tale end?
- Does the tale answer my question about nature?

Setting	Earth, in the beginning of time
Problem of the Story	Water needs more room for all the fish and animals that live in water.
Story Events	1. Water needs more room. 2. Sun and Moon make room for Water. 3. Water unintentionally floods Sun's and Moon's homes.
Solution to the Problem	Sun and Moon move to the sky so Water will have more room on Earth.

GLOSSARY

address   (uh-DRES) to speak to or write to directly (page 17)

content   (kun-TENT) satisfied (page 6)

grave   (GRAVE) serious; important (page 14)

matter   (MA-ter) a serious or unhappy situation (page 7)

minute   (my-NOOT) very small (page 8)

present   (PREH-zent) a gift (page 17)

racket   (RA-kut) a loud, confusing noise (page 13)

rose   (ROZE) moved upward (the past tense of rise) (page 20)

stand   (STAND) endure; hold out; tolerate (page 13)